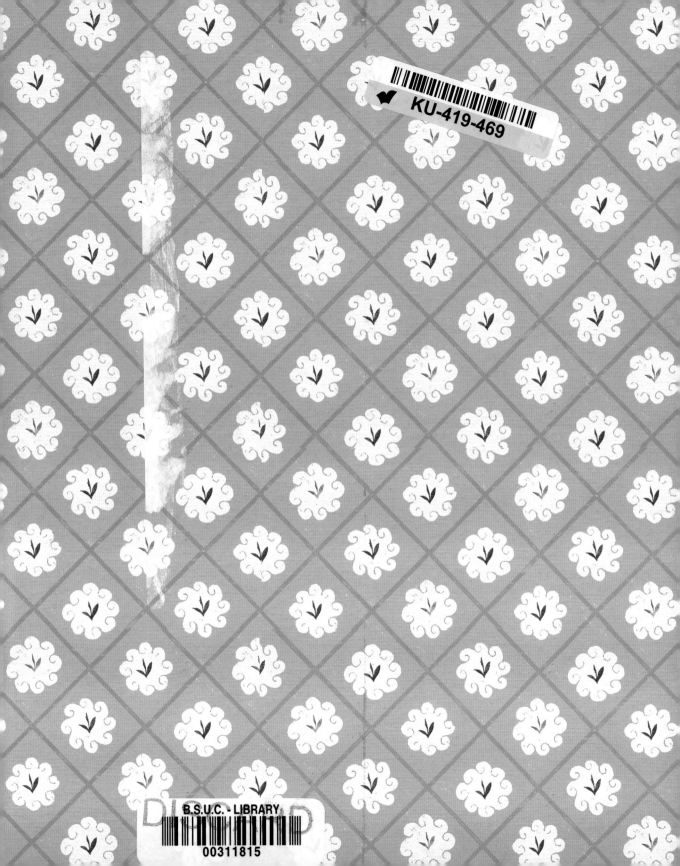

CLOUD TEA MONKEYS

For Vera
M. P. and E. G.

For Auntie Kitty
J. W.

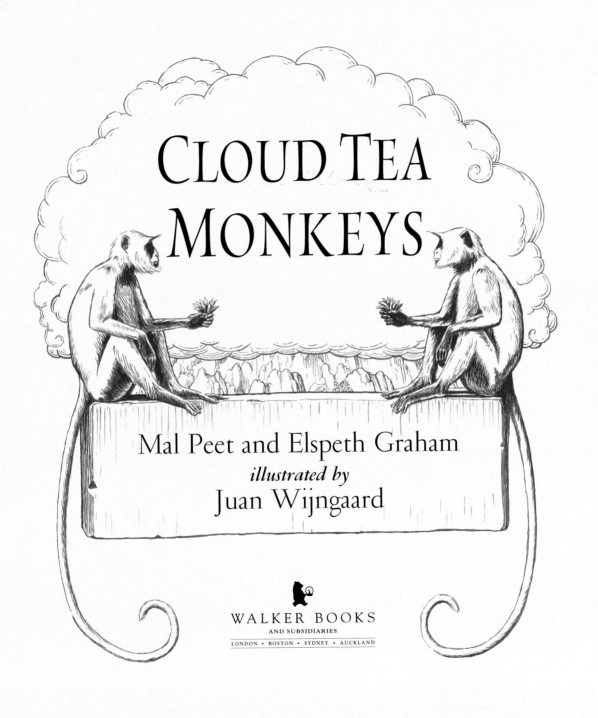

CLOUD TEA MONKEYS

Mal Peet and Elspeth Graham

illustrated by
Juan Wijngaard

WALKER BOOKS
AND SUBSIDIARIES
LONDON · BOSTON · SYDNEY · AUCKLAND

ONE BY ONE, the familiar sounds of morning drew Tashi from her sleep. Her mother breathing life into the fire; the hiss and crackle of the twigs as the flames caught; the whispering of the soot-blackened kettle as the water came to the boil.

Tashi took her bowl of sweet tea outside and stood beside the rough road in the blue morning. The sun had not yet found a way through the mountains, but it was coming; a light the colour of lemons was soaking into the sky and painting out the stars. The air was very cold. Tashi shivered and pulled her shawl more tightly around herself. As the stars went out, small squares of light appeared on the dark hillside above her: lamps were being lit in the village. A cockerel crowed and another answered. Inside the house her mother coughed, twice.

It was not long before they heard voices and laughter from where the road curved down from the hill. Then the women came, their white headscarves glowing in the half-dark, their clothes bright patches of scarlet, green, indigo. Each woman carried a great wicker basket, bigger than Tashi. They called her name, their voices wobbly in the cold air. Her mother came out of the house, her back bent under the burden of her tea-basket.

The walk to the tea plantation was long, but for Tashi this was a happy part of the day. The women gossiped and made jokes about their husbands. The sun was kind too, laying warm patches in the road that were good to walk into out of the cold shadows. Later the sun would turn cruel, burning down from a hazy sky.

When Tashi and her mother and the women arrived at the tea plantation the Overseer came out of his hut, yawning and scratching his belly. He was a bad-tempered man with a beaky nose and eyes like sharp little stones.

The women stood silently while he told them what they already knew, what they had always known: to pick only the young leaves and the buds from the tops of each bush. Then they found their places and began, plucking the tender leaves and buds and tossing them over their shoulders into their great wicker baskets.

The rows of glossy green tea bushes curved into the distance like waves. Tashi had never seen the end of the plantation. Perhaps it had no end. Perhaps it went right around the world.

Within an hour the sun had sucked the mist up out of the valleys and hung it like a great grey curtain over the tops of the mountains. Up there, on those wild mountain-tops above the cloud, were things Tashi was afraid of: big cats with jade-green eyes and snakes like yellow whips.

As usual the
monkeys came down into
the plantation late in the morning.
Tashi knew they had arrived when she heard
the Overseer shouting like a crazy man and beating a
tin cooking-pot with a stick to drive them away. The women
squealed and held their skirts tight to their legs as the monkeys,
showing their teeth in grins of fear, fled down the rows of bushes.
The big male monkey that Tashi called Rajah came first, then after
him the younger males, and after them the mothers with their
babies hanging beneath them or riding on their backs like jockeys
in a horse race. Tashi grabbed her lunch-bag and followed them.

Tashi and the monkeys met in their usual place, where the endless rows of tea bushes were broken by a jumble of rocks and a tree spread its shadow on the ground. Here she sat and crossed her legs. The monkeys watched her with their deep, serious eyes.

After a while the youngest ones left their mothers and came over to her. There was fruit in her lunch-bag and she shared it. The young monkeys inspected Tashi's fingers one by one. With their own long delicate fingers they groomed her thick dark hair. The mothers relaxed, trusting her. They snoozed in small groups or flirted with the young males. Rajah stalked around the edge of the tree-shadow, watching everything.

The women stopped work when the sun was a blurred red globe, hanging just above the rows of tea bushes. There was less talk on the way home. The women's tiredness was like a cloud around them. Tashi's mother had bruised-looking eyes. Her cough was worse. Once or twice she stopped walking and pressed her hand to her chest.

The next morning there was no crackle from the fire, no whisper from the kettle, no perfume of sweet tea.

"Tashi! Come here, child." Tashi crossed the dim room to her mother's bed. The cough was hard and sharp like a stick breaking. Her mother's face was cold but also wet with sweat.

"I am sick, child. I do not think I can work today."

Tashi ran to the dawn-lit road when she heard the women coming. Two came into the house: her Aunt Sonam and one other. They felt her mother's forehead and spoke to each other in low voices. Sonam brought water and told Tashi to make sure her mother drank. Then they hurried away to their work.

The next morning was the same. Tashi knew that if her mother could not work there would be no money. With no money to pay the doctor, her mother would not get well. If her mother did not get well, she could not work and there would be no money. The problem went round and round. It was like a snake with its tail in its mouth and Tashi was frightened by it.

When her mother was asleep again, Tashi dragged the heavy tea-basket to the door. She found that if she leant her body forward she could lift the bottom of the basket off the ground. Bent like this she began the long walk to the plantation.

When she got there Tashi could see no one; the bushes loomed above her. She could hear the shouts of the Overseer and the calls of the women. She hauled the basket along the rows until she saw Aunt Sonam plucking the bushes and dropping the leaves over her shoulder into her basket, over and over again, like a clockwork machine.

Before Tashi could reach Sonam, a shadow fell upon her. She looked up. The Overseer stood there, his hands on his hips. Desperately Tashi began to pick leaves, any leaves that she could reach.

The Overseer laughed an ugly laugh full of brown teeth. He called the other women to come and look at this stupid child who thought she could pick tea from bushes that were taller than herself. And then he kicked the basket over, spilling the sad and dusty leaves onto the ground. Tashi looked up into the face of her Aunt Sonam, but there was no help there. Sonam did not dare make an enemy of the Overseer, and she pulled an end of her headscarf over her face and turned away.

Tashi dragged the empty basket down to the shade of the tree that grew out of the rocks, and when she got there she sat and wept with her head in her hands. She wept for her mother and for Aunt Sonam and for herself. She cried for a long time. Then she wiped  her wet eyes with the backs of her hands and looked up. The monkeys were sitting in the circle of shade, watching her. They were all watching her – the babies hanging from their mothers, the older ones quiet for once, Rajah himself sitting looking at her with his old head tilted curiously to one side. So she told them everything. She told them everything because there was no one else to tell.

When she had finished there was stillness and silence for a few moments. Then Rajah walked through the tree-shadow towards her, coming closer than he had ever come before. He stood and was suddenly taller than Tashi. He put his long fingers on the rim of the basket and felt along it carefully. Then, without moving his head, he gave a harsh cry: *"Chack! Chack-chack-chack!"*

Instantly several of the adult monkeys leapt across the clearing, grabbed the basket, lifted it and then, with amazing strength and speed, carried it up and over the jumbled rocks towards the slopes of the mountains. Higher and higher they went, Rajah leading. In a very short time they and the basket had vanished into the clouds far above the plantation.

Tashi was too dismayed by the theft of her mother's basket to cry out. She stood watching the monkeys go, and then sat, feeling terribly tired. The young ones came to her. She took the three small bananas that were her lunch and shared them. Feeding the young ones calmed her. After a while she fell asleep.

She was awakened by a great outburst of screeching and whooping. The adults were back, and they were excited, bouncing from branch to rock and rock to branch, calling loudly. The young ones fled from Tashi's lap to their mothers; the mothers scolded the males for their madness. Rajah sat in the middle of the shade, ignoring all monkey business. He was watching Tashi. The basket stood beside him. She went to it and looked in.

The basket was almost full of small budding sprigs of tea and Tashi knew straight away that it was unusual. The leaves were the colour of emeralds and spangled with tiny droplets of water so that the basket seemed full of green light and a rich sweet scent.

The basket was even harder to manage now that it was full. It took Tashi a long time to drag it through the baking heat between the endless rows of bushes. When she came into the clearing around the Overseer's station, surprise stopped her dead. The tea-pickers were standing in a long line behind their baskets, whispering and giggling nervously.

Tashi hauled her basket over to where her aunt stood at the end of the line. Sonam looked down at the child with big astonished eyes but did not speak. The Overseer was marching about. He looked like a man whose brains were on fire. "Silence!" he yelled. "Silence! Stand straight! Be quiet!"

But it was not the Overseer's mad behaviour that interested Tashi. In the open space beside the hut was a cart with two wooden wheels. The two enormous oxen that had pulled it to the plantation stood twitching their tails at bothersome flies. The driver was a very small man wearing a white turban, and he seemed to be asleep.

In the cart there was a chair with cushions and a tall back, like a throne. It had a canopy of purple silk. And in the chair, in the purple shadow of the purple silk, sat a man made of silver light like the moon.

The Overseer spoke. "We are honoured," he said, "we are very, very honoured to be visited today by His Excellency the Royal Tea-Taster himself!" The Overseer turned and made a creepy crouching gesture towards the man who looked like the moon. "As you know, His Excellency the Royal Tea-Taster travels the whole world to find teas that are good enough to be drunk by Her Majesty the Empress!" The tea-pickers whispered to each other. The Overseer went dark in the face. "Silence! His Excellency the Royal Tea-Taster will now examine the tea in each of your baskets. And I am sure, quite sure, that he will find that the tea we grow on our plantation is the finest in the world."

The Royal Tea-Taster pulled himself up from his throne and stood in the sunlight. Now Tashi could see him clearly. Gold threads glittered in his blue turban, and his long white coat was so heavily embroidered with silver that it seemed to be made of white fire. His moustache was like a spread of snowy wings.

The Royal Tea-Taster strolled over to the line of women. He reached down into the first basket and picked out a sprig of tea. He held it up and looked at it very closely, frowning. He crushed the leaves and stuck his long nose into his cupped hands and sniffed a long, noisy sniff. Then he tossed the tea aside. He did this a few times along the line, but more often he just glanced at a basket of tea and moved on. The Overseer followed at a respectful distance, his hands rubbing each other, his face wearing a sick and frightened grin.

The Royal Tea-Taster was quite close to Sonam and Tashi when the Overseer lost control of himself and dared to speak.

"Excellency, sir!" he said. "This tea, our tea: it is very fine, is it not? Is it not a most beautiful tea?"

The Royal Tea-Taster lifted his nose as if he had smelt a dead rat.

"Your tea," he said, "your tea is ... ordinary."

The Overseer moaned and bent almost double as if he had a great pain in his stomach.

The Royal Tea-Taster moved on and at last stood before Sonam and Tashi. Tashi looked up into his eyes, which were almost as deep and dark as the eyes of Rajah.

The Royal Tea-Taster turned to walk away. Then he stopped. His nose twitched.

He came back to the basket that stood in front of Tashi and dipped his plump hand into it, testing the warm dampness of the leaves. He took a single sprig and studied it, twirling it between his fingers. He crushed it and sniffed it, twice.

"Where did you pick this?"

He spoke to Sonam, not to Tashi.

Sonam said, "Sir, I did not pick it. This child did. Her name is Tashi. She is the daughter of my sister, who is sick."

The Royal Tea-Taster took a step back so that he could see Tashi over the gleaming bulge of his belly. His look was very stern. He lifted a hand and clicked his fingers.

The tiny sleeping man on the cart immediately woke up, jumped to the ground and ran first to the back of the cart and then across to where the Royal Tea-Taster stood. In one hand he carried a leather bag and in the other a small iron dish of burning charcoal, trailing smoke. He set the dish of charcoal on the ground and took from the bag a small copper kettle and a silver flask. He poured water from the flask into the kettle and sat the kettle on the fire and blew furiously onto the charcoal until it burned red.

The lid of the kettle rattled when the water boiled. The little man – who was in fact the Deputy Chief Tea-Boiler – reached into the bag again and took out a milk-white porcelain bowl. It was so thin that Tashi could see the shadow of the little man's fingers through it. He put three sprigs of Tashi's tea into the bowl, poured boiling water onto them and handed the bowl to the Royal Tea-Taster. The Royal Tea-Taster held the bowl close to his nose and bent over. The little man then covered the Royal Tea-Taster's head and the bowl with a white cloth. Tashi wanted to giggle but did not dare.

There was silence for several moments. Then from under the cloth there came a good deal of sniffing and snuffling: short shallow snuffles and then some long deep sniffs and then the kind of gasping that comes before a sneeze. Then another, longer silence. A hand came out from under the cloth. The fingers clicked again and the little man reached up and lifted the cloth from the Royal Tea-Taster's head.

When Tashi saw his face, the Royal Tea-Taster no longer looked stern; he looked like a man who had seen an angel. He lifted the bowl to his lips and sucked in tea with a tremendous snorty slurping sound, which made Tashi jump. He rolled the tea around inside his mouth, first one cheek bulging, then the other. He opened his mouth slightly and drew in more air, gurgling. Then he turned his head and – *pfft!* – spat the tea onto the ground. Now he stood still with his eyes closed, breathing in and out through his mouth.

At last the Royal Tea-Taster opened his eyes and sighed a sigh of pure joy. His smile was like the sun rising out of the mountains as he beamed down at Tashi.

"Come with me," he said.

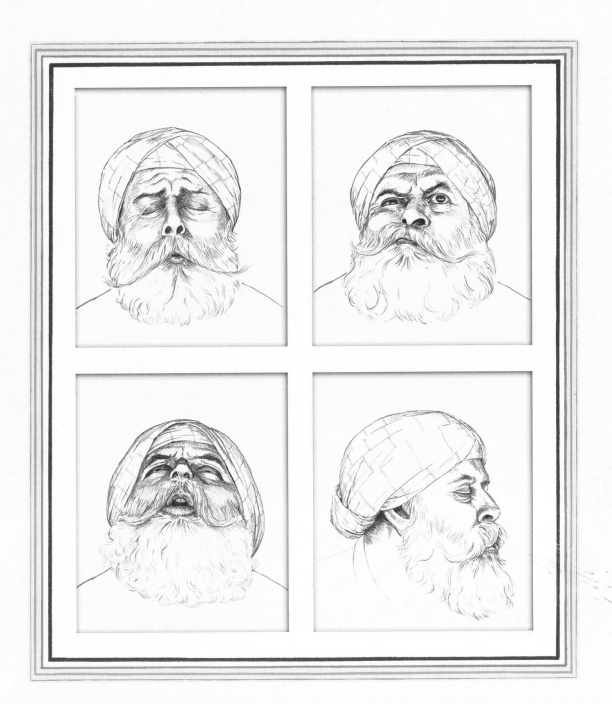

He took her by the hand and together they walked over to the ox-cart. The Royal Tea-Taster studied the small anxious child who stood before him.

"In my life," he said, "I have tasted many, many kinds of tea. Perhaps a thousand kinds of tea. But until today I had tasted Cloud Tea only twice, and the last time was many years ago. And you know why, don't you?"

Tashi said nothing because she could not think of anything to say.

"Of course you know. You know that Cloud Tea is almost impossible to find and even more difficult to pick, because it grows up there." He pointed a finger up to where the mountains were wrapped in cloud. "It is the most magical and delicious tea in the world but it grows wild in high, dangerous places where men are afraid to go." He bent down to Tashi and spoke in a softer voice. "So I ask myself this: how could a small child have gathered this tea? Tell me, are you able to fly?"

Tashi lowered her eyes. Her tongue felt too big for her mouth. She knew that if she told this man the truth he would not believe her. She wondered if she was still asleep and dreaming.

"No, sir," she said. "I cannot fly."

"So. A small child cannot tell the Royal Tea-Taster how she found the most valuable tea in the world. Is that correct?"

Tashi said, "Yes." It was the hardest thing she'd ever had to say. The Royal Tea-Taster nodded seriously. "Very well," he said. "I have my secrets too." And then he smiled. "Come closer," he said, "and listen carefully. In exactly one year from today I will come here again. And I will come here again the year after that, and every year after that. And each time I come here I want you to bring me a basket of Cloud Tea. And each time you bring me a basket of Cloud Tea I will give you one of these."

He held out a silk pouch that was small but heavy. Tashi took it, opened it and looked inside. The coins were fat and made of gold, and there were many of them.

Just one of those fat gold coins was enough to pay the doctor who came up from the city to the tiny house on the mountain. The cough that sounded like sticks breaking went away and Tashi's mother grew strong again. But she did not go back to the plantation to work every day under the hot eye of the sun.

A year later, just one of the fat gold coins was also enough to pay for fruit to fill the tea-basket: juicy mangoes, sleek bananas, red-jewelled pomegranates, the rosiest of apples, the most perfect of peaches. In the shadow of the tree that grew from the jumbled rocks, the monkeys feasted.

And afterwards, while Tashi dozed with the babies on her lap, Rajah and the big monkeys stole away up the mountain with the empty basket and brought it back filled with the magical green glow of Cloud Tea.

Later, the ox-cart came; a plump hand reached out of the purple shade and dropped a plump silk pouch into Tashi's palm.

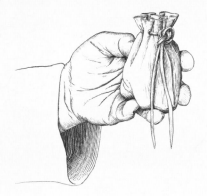

There are only three people in the world who drink Cloud Tea. One of them is a little old woman who is called the Empress of All the Known World and Other Bits That Have Not Been Discovered Yet. The other two are a retired tea-picker and her daughter, who live in a village among mountains whose tops are lost in clouds.

❧ Authors' Note ❧

Many of the simple things we can buy easily and cheaply today in shops were once rare and precious. Merchants undertook hard, dangerous journeys to find and trade goods like salt, spices, sugar, cocoa – and tea.

Our story was inspired by this, and by the many tea-picking tales we found from the high mountain countries of the Himalayan region – where the finest tea grows. One tale tells of monkeys who were taught to pick tea by monks. Another tells of farmers who drove monkeys away from their villages, and when the angry monkeys threw sticks back, the farmers discovered that the leaves on them made a wonderful drink.

Cloud Tea Monkeys *is set in the past, but you can still buy "monkey-picked tea", though whether or not it is really picked by monkeys is another story again...*

❧ *Mal Peet and Elspeth Graham* ❧

First published 2010 by Walker Books Ltd
87 Vauxhall Walk, London SE11 5HJ

2 4 6 8 10 9 7 5 3

Text © 1999, 2010 Mal Peet and Elspeth Graham
Illustrations © 2010 Juan Wijngaard

The right of Mal Peet and Elspeth Graham and Juan Wijngaard
to be identified as authors and illustrator respectively of this work
has been asserted by them in accordance with the
Copyright, Designs and Patents Act 1988

This book has been typeset in Garamond Ludlow.

Printed in China

British Library Cataloguing in Publication Data:
a catalogue record for this book
is available from the British Library

ISBN 978-1-4063-0092-5

www.walker.co.uk